The Little Match Girl

D1634768

700030424112

First published in 2006 by
Franklin Watts
338 Euston Road
London
NW1 3BH

Franklin Watts Australia
Hachette Children's Books
Level 17/207 Kent Street
Sydney
NSW 2000

A CIP catalogue record for this book is available
from the British Library.

ISBN 0 7496 6576 9 (hbk)
ISBN 0 7496 6582 3 (pbk)

Series Editor: Jackie Hamley
Series Advisor: Dr Barrie Wade
Series Designer: Peter Scoulding

Printed in China

For Leonora – H.R.

The Little Match Girl

Retold by Hilary Robinson

Illustrated by Shelagh McNicholas

FRANKLIN WATTS
LONDON·SYDNEY

It was a cold
winter evening.

A poor little girl was
trying to earn money
by selling matches.

As the sun set, party lights
lit up in the windows.

The little match girl
huddled behind a wall
to keep warm.

"If I light just one match,"
she said, "I could warm
my frozen feet."

In the flame, the little match girl saw a warm fireplace.

But as she tried to warm her feet, the flame flickered and went out.

The little match girl struck another match. In the flame she saw a feast.

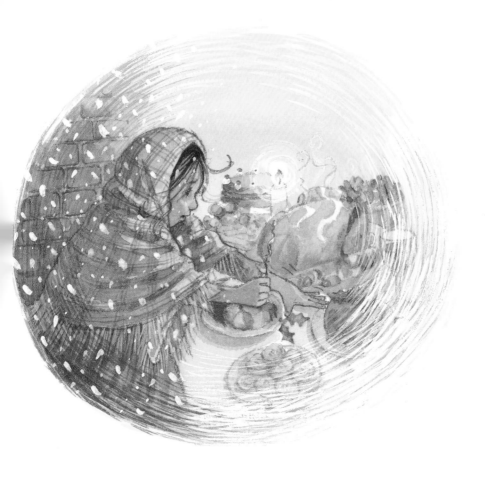

But as she reached for the
food, the flame flickered
and went out.

She struck another match. This time she found herself sitting under a glittering Christmas tree.

As the flame flickered
and went out, the light
from a candle rose up
and became a trail
of a twinkling star.

"That means that someone
is dying," thought the little
match girl.

Her granny used to say,

"When a star falls, someone

is going to heaven."

The fourth time she lit a match, she saw her granny smiling at her.

"Please take me with you,
Granny," she pleaded.
"I miss you."

The next day, as the sun rose, a lifeless body of a little girl lay by the wall.

"Poor girl," said the
passers-by. "She must
have been icy cold."

But the little match girl
was now warm and happy
in a faraway place ...

... where she shone
like starlight.

Leapfrog has been specially designed to fit the requirements of the National Literacy Strategy. It offers real books for beginning readers by top authors and illustrators.

There are 49 Leapfrog stories to choose from:

* hardback